I0725999

Island Woman

Rosey Thomas Palmer

Published by

Dayglo Books Ltd, Nottingham, UK

www.dayglobooks.co.uk

0019-15-1816-01

Cover artwork & illustrations by
www.valentineart.co.uk

Typeset in Opendyslexic
by Abelardo Gonzales (2013)

Printed by IngramSpark

Distributed by Filament Publishing Ltd, Croydon

Foreword

The women of the island of Jamaica are strong, proud and beautiful.

Their strength has come down to them, over the generations. They have survived years of hard and sometimes bitter times.

The original inhabitants of Jamaica – the Taino people – watched their homeland endure many invasions.

Caribs came from neighbouring islands. The Taino suffered raids by marauding sea captains from Spain. Taino land was taken by ambitious

English settlers. The Taino felt the grief of African slaves brought unwillingly to work on the plantations.

Gradually the Taino people withdrew from the sea shore and the fertile lowlands. They gathered in their last stronghold – the rocky uplands of the island. Here was a secret system of inter-connected underground caves.

They were joined by some few who risked terrible punishment to cast off the shackles of slavery and run away. Together, in the uplands, they lived as free people, known as the Maroon.

One modern Jamaican woman sought out her history – Taino, Spanish, Maroon and slave. This book tells the moving story of one of her foremothers who was named Zeesha.

"The names in our bloodline have taught me that women are not to be oppressed. There is pride and belonging in a remembered name. It has the power to call home a traveller who may have forgotten her way."

Island Woman

Jamaica, 1660

Chapter 1 – In the Cave

In the Cave of Great Gatherings, Zeesha squatted among the other adolescent girls of her own age.

Zeesha was tall, slender, and dark skinned. In looks, she took after her father, Quashy.

Among the older women sat Zeesha's grandmother.

She had glowing, russet skin. Her kinked hair hung in longer fronds than most. Her cheeks carried the breadth of the ancient people.

She was the mother of Quashy, Zeesha's father.

Quashy had two younger brothers, named Koyot and Ku. These men were Zeesha's uncles.

Zeesha's grandmother was the great-grand-daughter of their revered ancestor, Esther.

She had called her son Ku, after Esther's son of the same name.

Legend taught how Esther had loved a man named Quincy – an adventurer and visionary.

Quincy had left the knowledge of
many places and many cultures to the
upland people.

He had gleaned this knowledge
from his own travels. Also from his
musings on hundreds of years of trade
and conflict with the countries of the
far north.

The tale told how, together, Esther
and Quincy had planned to create
a race of free people.

These ancestors were remembered
with great respect. They were loved
and admired for the wisdom they had
given their people.

Chapter 2 - The Gathering

Today, all Zeesha's family held positions of responsibility among the upland people. They would all speak at the gathering today.

The people sat in a circle, within a ring of tall stones, waiting.

The teenage girls were at the outside of the circle. The women of childbearing age were to their right, and towards the centre were the older women.

On the other side of the cave, the men stood in rank.

Those in greatest authority were at the centre, with the warriors to their right. The young men were placed farthest away from the young women.

They were poised, keen and attentive, as they waited for their leader.

He would come and sit high above them. He would sit on a ledge of rock on the side of the Cave of Great Gatherings.

All those who were dedicated to the peace of their homeland had come to the cave today.

As she waited, Zeesha allowed her eyes to wander over the patient throng.

They had come from all over the uplands of her island home. They came from the mountain tops, which whitened cool with mist at dawn.

They came from steep slopes, where they had to cut the land into steps to make it fruitful.

They came from the upland valleys, rich in ferns and fruits of all kinds. And they came from the rolling plateaux that the sun baked hard as terra-cotta pots.

'No one from the plains', she noticed.

The people seemed to have split into two camps – those who wanted to stay in their beautiful island home and those who did not.

Zeesha knew that her great-great-great-grandmother, Esther, had had to make that choice long ago.

That was when the Europeans had first started to squabble amongst themselves for the land.

Now it seemed certain that, whatever side you were on, you could lose your inheritance.

The rich, tropical forest and warm, gentle sea were at stake.

There was danger, if you mixed with the harsh, warring factions of those northern nations.

Chapter 3 - Reports

At last, the leader came, dressed in a colourful robe. In fact, Zeesha only thought of him as their leader at these great meetings. For all the rest of the time, he was simply her uncle, Ku.

He greeted the people.

"Co-ay," he called to each group, and they shouted "Co-ay!" back. Then it was time to get down to business.

Runners came forward and made their reports.

The first told how the few remaining Spaniards had been seen at scattered ports. They were loading up their great ships to depart. A flotilla had gathered off the north coast. The ships trimmed their sails to the breeze that would carry them home.

Others reports spoke of sheltered inlets around the island. Here, the English had been seen. They slipped in at night on their small, swift craft.

More reports told how groups of men with metal hats and breastplates were closing in on the remaining Spanish strongholds.

These men moved with speed and discipline. They amazed even the most seasoned guerrilla fighters of the uplands.

Witnesses told the gathering how coastal settlements had been raided and burned. They told how many men, women and children had lost their lives already. These deadly incursions were by British forces.

At last, Zeesha's uncle Ku took charge. He acknowledged the reports but told them to stop mulling over past events and turn their minds towards how to proceed now.

There was a rustling in the ranks at his words. Several people hissed with resentment. But generally the mood of the meeting was practical. They all needed to survive the changes that the newcomers brought.

Some warriors, just out of their youth, put forward an idea.

They thought a big convergence of all the island people would overcome the British. They could compel them to return home, like the Spaniards.

More seasoned men thought differently.

They believed that harassing them continually would destabilise them and cause them to retreat.

Some, who thought themselves particularly wise and sober, said no.

They said that the hot, tropical conditions and insects would be their own solution to this new invasion.

They pointed out how the Spaniards had always remained on the plains and left the interior to the true islanders.

When all these views had been expressed, it was then that Zeesha's father, Quashy, addressed the crowd.

Chapter 4 – The Spitting Fire

Standing respectfully before his younger brother Ku, Quashy spoke.

Zeesha's heart grew with pride as she listened to her father.

He was a skilful man, an inventor, with a creative mind.

It was not easy for him to hold his own at such gatherings. He had to speak forcefully and emphasise his individual point of view.

He had to distance himself. He had

to stand, mentally, outside of the gathering and speak his own mind.

"The last speaker said what was right, according to our history and our experience," Quashy began.

"But suppose the new intruders are not like us? Suppose they are unlike the Spaniards, too?

"Suppose they are like the Caribs, who eradicated my great-great-grand-mother's people from surrounding shores?

"Suppose they come not to share, but to possess?"

"How do we know what these men intend?" Quashy pressed.

"They are not of our ways or of our culture. Should we leave ourselves open to discover the truth by death and destruction?

"This is what the ancient people did before us.

"They discovered that these newcomers have no reverence for the land, or for those who have inhabited it before them."

Time and time again, indeed, such points had proved well-founded.

This time, Quashy had received a low grunt of approval from the elders.

Then Koyot stood. He was the proven leader of the warriors. He was also brother to Ku and Quashy.

He was always impatient about Quashy's public urgings.

He had over-ridden his brother's views before, by more popular suggestions about guerrilla warfare.

Today, Koyot was defiant.

"If they try to advance into our territory, we will repulse them," he declared.

Koyot held influence over their fighting force of warriors.

"But that is not the objective," Quashy persisted. "The objective is to understand their intentions. And what they propose to do to our land."

As he said this, a murmur of fury rose from the warrior ranks.

Quashy was patient and brave as he faced them.

"What we need," he said quietly, "is more technology. Their ships are swifter than ours. They carry more men than ours. They spit fire and destroy approaching vessels.

"One day, they will learn how to hold the spitting fire in their hands and throw it at us. It could happen here, even in our hallowed uplands.

"We need to know how the fire is made, in order to quench it!

"Some of their technology may baffle us, but we have to take an interest. They may have the power to rob us, and our children, of our freedom if we do not come to understand them."

Chapter 5 – Counsel from an Elder

The warriors grew silent. The older women stirred. From among their ranks a woman stood.

It was Zeesha's grandmother.

"Whilst my mother was raising me," she began, "my great-grand-mother, Esther, taught me. She sat me many times on that very rock where you stand now, Koyot. She spoke to me long and intently.

"She told me about the nature of Spanish commerce. She told me about world communication. About the ships that ply between continents we have no thought of.

"She told me how they bring messages across oceans. They transmit things of value to enrich people who have not known each other.

"I counsel you, my grandson, to listen to Quashy, your elder brother.

"You should seek a way to learn about these cold-blooded people before they raise forces against us that we cannot combat."

A hush now settled on the gathering.

Koyot was clearly perplexed. His brow gathered, though his lips were firm.

"We will seek the means of attaining this knowledge," he said, "though to get it may prove very costly."

"I will bear the cost," Quashy announced.

The crowd fell silent at his words.

"Let us withdraw privately and we will counsel the leader accordingly," Zeesha's grandmother said solemnly.

Ku rose, as if beckoned by the voice of his mother.

The bright hues of his ceremonial robe unfolded around him as he stood.

"Warfare will wait," he said. "This is a time for cunning. We will seek knowledge."

Chapter 6 – The Decision

Zeesha knew that her grandmother loved each of her three sons fiercely.

She valued the power of Ku. She treasured the forethought of Quashy. And she admired the prowess of Koyot.

Zeesha remembered the tales of Esther, who had loved Quincy.

Quincy had rejected the confines of servitude, and regained his freedom. He had created new links with an older race of people. He was keen to ensure that he and his descendants would be able to continue to live in peace, when the Spaniards left their temporary colony.

Quashy and Ku were Quincy's successors. They were leaders now. They believed it was time to stop responding defensively to change. Instead, they felt they should make a plan to meet it boldly.

Ku felt unwilling to come to a decision in the open council. There, he felt pushed by Koyot and his warriors. He preferred to listen to the views of his mother, explained privately.

Knowing this, Zeesha became very quiet. She wanted to hear what her elders said to each other.

She loved listening to the tossing back and forth of ideas. She was excited by new knowledge.

She knew how to make herself inconspicuous and let them forget that she was there.

First, she supplied them with bamboo cups filled with maize wine. She ensured that a coil of chewing tobacco lay handy.

She settled on a mat, just within earshot. She hugged Koyot's youngest baby girl between her knees. She began to plait the child's hair into fine spirals around her scalp.

"What is it you really want?" Koyot asked Quashy. "Do you want to know whether they have come to stay? Or do

you want to learn how to throw fire
yourself?"

"Both!" Quashy replied.

"Whether they plan to settle here
has direct consequences for our people.

"If they are the sole guardians of
the secret of the throwing fire, matters
will be settled by them, with no
reference to us."

"They only throw the fire at sea,"
Koyot objected. "How could that
concern us? We are not planning to
leave here.

"If we had wanted to go, we would
have taken our canoes long ago. We
could have followed the old folk. We
could have slipped away to join others
of their race across the water."

"We have only seen them use the fire over the sea," Quashy corrected. "That does not mean they could not adapt its use to the land."

"That is highly unlikely," Koyot scoffed. "How could they risk the fire falling on dry vegetation, or even on houses?

"It would take on a will of its own. It would burn wherever the wind blows it. At sea, it is contained by the water. So it affects only its intended target."

Chapter 7 – The Sacrifice

"Listen and co-operate."

It was her grandmother's voice. It was partly obscured by chewing. But it had a soothing and compulsive tone, nonetheless.

"The people who came together in us did not survive by pitting their minds and their energies against each other," she counselled. "They survived by combining their wisdom and skills."

Koyot breathed deeply and started again.

"You say we must get to know what their intentions are. How do you propose we do that?"

"By watching them from afar," Quashy replied.

Ku spoke with the dignity of his position.

"We have been doing that. It has not minimised the frequency of their raids. Nor has it altered their intention to establish lasting settlements."

"Then we must infiltrate them," Quashy said quickly, as if he had been waiting for this opening.

"How? These men are surly and brutal. We cannot repeat the mistakes made by the old folks long ago. We cannot risk more massacres and repeated slavery."

"We cannot risk more suicides, either, by letting them take our land and rob us of our lifestyle," Quashy agreed. He entered into the rhythm of the exchange.

Koyot remembered Quashy's final statement at the public gathering.
'I will bear the cost,' Quashy had said.

"What will be the cost of our resolution?" Koyot asked him.

"Zeesha," said her father.

Zeesha's fingers froze in her cousin's hair. The style she was creating would never be completed.

"It is not a new thought," came her grandmother's crooning voice.

"Quashy and I have shared it before."

"Why sacrifice a girl? What can a girl do?" Koyot demanded.

"Don't exaggerate," Quashy scoffed. "These are not the days of Taino and Carib warfare. She won't be killed or confined for showing a little island hospitality."

Zeesha's grandmother spoke:

"It has always been a woman's role to soften the invader with invitations to idleness."

Her words of betrayal were honey to the men's ears.

"We will be constantly in touch with her through the network of caves," Quashy persisted.

"I have my reservations, but if it is the will of the gathering then I agree, if we respond cautiously," Ku conceded. "And I cannot commit the child of any other family."

"She will be honoured to play as great a role for our people as Esther played before her."

Her grandmother's seal on Zeesha's fate was an intoxicant to her sons.

They were so convinced by this argument they could not wait to implement the decision.

They cherished the notion that Zeesha could do for her generation what Esther and Quincy had done for theirs.

Chapter 8 – Personal Honour

Across the intervening years, Zeesha often wondered how her own father could have betrayed her.

He had persuaded her to accept his suggestion in so many ways. He told her it was a personal honour for her.

He told her it was a necessary means of securing his position in the community.

He told her it was the only practical solution to the threat of a new invasion.

He told her it was a temporary service to her people.

Whatever his reasoning may have been, she felt rejected and dejected.

She wondered if her Taino origins made her less necessary to her community than the other girls. Or if her Spanish descent made her more expendable.

She hoped that her role as a spy did justice to her keen intelligence.

However, in view of this strange assignment, she felt having intelligence was a mixed blessing.

The most comforting realisation that came to her was that she had a quick tongue. She could grasp and convey the meanings she heard with accuracy. This soothed her and led her to believe her venture would be a success.

Zeesha was accompanied to the mouth of the cave, on the coastal plain, and told to advance alone.

She shivered for the last time. Pride and secrecy would be her only disguise.

Chapter 9 – The Newcomers

She walked out into the dim of twilight and headed, as she had been told, for the wood fires of two soldier brothers.

She heard their foreign voices and the snap of twigs as they moved around their temporary encampment.

Like many others who had taken their discharge from Cromwell's rabble army, they knew little of how to survive here. The mosquitoes would be biting them mercilessly down here, so near the swamp.

She listened to their shuffling, moaning complaints as the night deepened.

Though the sounds of the night were a lullaby to her, they produced restless cries of frustration from the newcomers.

She strained through the night to distinguish their voices and their personalities.

She decided to make herself known to the gentler of the two first. She would then trust him to introduce her to the other one.

It seemed to her, they were brothers.

Dawn was her best chance. Then, they would separate to prepare themselves for the day.

The one she had chosen for her protection would be able to argue for her safety. He would be able to give examples of her usefulness.

So Zeesha made sure that she was observed.

First, she set out bamboos for a hut. Next she went fishing in a stream.

She was not alarmed when she was interrupted kindling a fire before she was able to cook the catch.

The voice was rough and indistinct, but clearly, he wanted to join her.

He was young. Droplets of water from the stream still clung to his beard. At least, he was clean.

She motioned for him to sit. She slit open the fish with her flint knife, preparing it for roasting.

She deliberately did not notice how he watched her.

When the fish was done, she gave him a piece to taste, but then his companion's voice sounded. She quickly kicked out the fire and ran.

Chapter 10 – Separation

The men may have wanted to pursue her, but Zeesha did not wait to find out.

She hid at the entrance to the cave. She decided to sleep there, as long as they were within a half day's travel from it.

Thus, though they thought they stalked her, she stalked them.

Zeesha learned their language as they learned survival. She lingered on the outskirts of their lives.

She delighted in tantalizing the one brother. She interacted very little with the other.

The two men met with little resistance. Aside, that was from the harsh, noon-day sun. And the predator insects, which inflamed their flesh.

The streams were clean, the fish plentiful, and the fruit in abundance.

The strangers became more content.

As they did so, their observer became more frustrated.

Zeesha concluded that it was beneath her dignity to return to the upland community without information.

She had heard her uncles speak about their technology with fire. But she had seen two men less expert at starting fires than she was. And less proficient at building shelters

They seemed in no hurry to go away. But they had no interest in occupying the former Spanish settlements.

They were forever standing and viewing the terrain.

They knew she was there, so they must have expected other inhabitants to be on the island. Yet they showed no curiosity about seeking them out.

They lived off the land from day to day. They showed a lively interest in nothing, except the occasional herd of cattle and horses that roamed by, grazing the lush, lowland grass.

Eventually, Zeesha saw the two men beginning to separate. Her favourite tended towards the upland slopes. The other man liked to remain on the plain.

This suited her. She wound her way back and forth through the length of the cave. This was where she had been left by her people, at the opening.

The attractive stranger began to pace the area outside the cave every day, as if to establish a boundary.

She watched both men, until she saw the one who preferred the coast go to seek contact with others like him.

They rowed along the shore in cumbersome canoes. They had long paddles that lay wide as they dipped through the water.

The man's preoccupation with the newcomers would be her chance. She could draw closer to the attractive one now, without being observed.

During her period of hiding, Zeesha had been able to calm her hurt feelings. She was as resilient and hopeful as all the girls of her community.

And she had watched this man closely in his most secret moments.

She had noticed the cleanliness with which he kept himself, even in these unknown surroundings. She had heard him whistle softly and sing to himself, when the other man was out of earshot.

She had been reassured by his evident delight on the few occasions when they had met face-to-face.

She was supremely confident in her environment. He was a novice.

She was the representative of an ordered community. He was isolated.

But he was a man, and she had begun to like him.

Chapter 11 – The Wooing

It was a delicate, secret wooing. She demonstrated the art of weaving the tallest bamboos to create shade from the sun. He let her observe him openly.

She touched his hair and rubbed aloe into his sunburned shoulders. But she skipped away before he caught her hand.

He spoke to her, and she did not understand. He smiled, and she did.

One day, he reached under his tunic and took out a moon-coloured stick, like a bamboo stem, and waved it in her face.

She wondered if that was what she had come to find. But before she could learn anything else about it, he had laughed and put it away.

She thought she would search for it in his clothes the next time he bathed, but he seemed to have read her mind. He always left his things on the far side of the bank.

The deadlock broke one day. She had been stalking him, while he stalked a stray cow from the Spanish herd. She saw him pull out the bamboo stick again and make it suddenly flash.

The loud noise of the explosion terrified her. She began to run, but then turned to look back. She wanted to see if he had set fire to the cow. Her uncle had said the technology did that to ships.

The turn threw her off balance, and she sprawled against a tree root.

The man did the most peculiar thing. He came to look at her where she had fallen. He bent down beside her like a mother to her child. He put his hand on her twisted foot.

His voice, when he spoke to her, was like the quiet song he sung when he was alone.

Tingling with excitement and pleasure, Zeesha fluttered her eyelids and used every ounce of her womanly charms to subtly enquire about his amazing magic.

He smiled and reassured her that she would have all the time in the world to learn about his technology. He told her that he would be willing to share many secrets.

The time they spent together seemed to pass slowly. Their combined skills provided a sweet, quiet way of life.

He was intent on herding the cattle he had seen on the plain into wide enclosures. Zeesha considered this exhausting and unnecessary.

But she knew how to create a home of bamboo and thatch. She knew how to catch fish, select fruit, and cook 'bammy' – the flat, unleavened bread she made from the starchy cassava plant. So she occupied herself with everyday chores.

She watched for information about the intentions of these newcomers. She learned, from him, to understand their language.

She worried when he went off for a day or so at a time to the coastal plain to visit his former companion.

Chapter 12 – Naming of Strangers

She took advantage of these absences to go home. She climbed carefully down the shaft in the cave and made her way through the underground passages. She was glad to find members of her community – people she could trust with the information she had gleaned from him.

The elders were much reassured. They were content to let her continue her life with him. However, they had heard less favourable news of the settlement that was arising along the coast.

They felt that having at least one friendly presence would help to adjust the balance of power when the time came. They especially wanted her to learn the secret of the fire weapon and secure one for them.

There were more fears about the arrival on the coast of groups of unhealthy Africans. They were being forcibly taken to occupy the newly settled lands.

There was more concern about this than about Zeesha's well-being.

In spite of temporary happiness, Zeesha did not entirely share the complacency of her people.

She watched her young man as carefully as she ever had. She learned his name was Luke Copperwright, and his brother was called Peter.

She felt a deep fondness for Luke. However, she did not perceive their life together as secure.

She knew the importance of close family ties between the generations, and across the generations.

She was aware that babies could be born to them, all too soon. She realised that this would endanger their self-sufficiency.

She would never reveal to him the numbers or the whereabouts of her own people. This would have betrayed their trust and stood in the way of their continued support.

Neither would she willingly withdraw to them in her time of need.

She feared that a child fathered by Luke Copperwright might feel rejected by her people the in future.

She remembered how rejected she had felt, when she had been selected for this task.

Yet she knew he was far too vulnerable to protect her when the weight of motherhood was upon her. Or when she was immersed in the demands of a new-born.

Sometimes, she wondered whether worries about their future haunted Luke Copperwright also.

Sometimes he shivered as the sun went down. Or perhaps it was her own fears she was seeing, on those occasions.

Chapter 13 – Relocation

Zeesha was almost sure it must be a coincidence that they were both unwell at the same time.

She felt a tingling in her breasts and drowsy sickness in the mornings. At night, he suffered alternate shivering and periods of intense body heat.

As his conditioned worsened, she fought off her own weariness at night.

Zeesha was alarmed by Luke's restlessness.

She was disturbed by the need to cool his overheated body.

Sometimes, he seemed to see things she could not see. He would talk to people who were not there.

From time to time a few retainers of the departed Spanish came across to the place where she stayed with Luke. They wanted to share Luke's dream and seek their fortunes.

In spite of this, life became harder to sustain on their little settlement. Luke said they should go to stay with his brother Peter, where there were more people.

Zeesha would have liked to take Luke to her own community in the hills. But they told her they were not prepared for her to reveal them to the newcomers yet.

However, she asked and accepted the advice of the older women about herbs that would help Luke's condition.

She also received from the women a goat-skin bag containing a curious object.

It was a rounded, godlike, talisman, known as a 'zemi'. It lay in the bag among some dried leaves.

Her uncles Ku and Koyot were glad about her relocation with Luke to his brother Peter's house. Now Zeesha would bring them news from the rapidly growing coastal settlement.

It would be more use than the hints she had been able to pass on from the secluded spot where she stayed with Luke Copperwright.

The coastal settlement had grown almost beyond recognition.

There were some members of the invading forces who had remained. In addition, there were many who had come and set up businesses.

There were ships' chandlers, who imported necessary supplies, such as rope, tar and canvas. There were shops selling foodstuffs, such as ships' biscuits and salt fish.

The chandlers serviced ships that passed on their way to and from other islands, and the newly settled continent of America.

They were eager for those who claimed land on the coastal plains to grow other provisions, such as limes and oranges. These would help to keep the crew and passengers of the vessels healthy on long voyages.

Fruit was in great demand. So were the cattle that Luke Copperwright drove down from the hills.

Some were penned on board ship. Others were slaughtered, wholesale, to be stored in barrels with brine to preserve the flesh. Fat and hides were also horded.

Zeesha now understood the reason for Luke Copperwright's enterprise.

But she was sickened by such a waste of life. She wondered how many people must be packed into those multi-storey vessels to consume so much food.

Her questioning led her to the sad sight of groups of dejected Africans. They were herded ashore from the ships, in the same way that the cattle were herded on to them.

Zeesha saw money changing hands. Then the Africans were led off, in the wake of horsemen. They were heading for the outlying lands to which the purchasers had laid claim.

Chapter 14 – Men of Wealth

Many of the horsemen leading the slaves came and went, to and from Peter Copperwright's new dwelling. This place became Luke and Zeesha's temporary home.

By listening to the brothers' conversations with their visitors, Zeesha learned much about their intentions.

They spoke of gold, either with disappointment or anticipation. Some wanted to travel further afield to places where they could dig it up. Others wanted to generate it through commerce.

Peter Copperwright spoke of growing it in the form of a grass-like plant called sugar cane.

Zeesha wondered what a society of so few people, concerned only with self-adornment, could want with so much gold.

It seemed to represent wealth to them, and that was their favourite topic of conversation.

Peter and Luke Copperwright quarrelled frequently about the means to achieve wealth.

Peter called Luke's cattle ranch ingenious but short-lived. Luke said that

Peter's plans for a plantation were grandiose and exploitative.

Luke's passion for freedom was burning, but when he argued in the evening, he became fevered at night.

As Luke grew physically weaker, Peter became more strident, more over-bearing. He turned his tenderness for his brother's weakness to belittling scorn.

Zeesha, silent and watchful in the background, heard and learned. She saw the power seeping from the brother she had chosen.

"Your hillside cattle ranch is just a starter project," Peter would say. "The prospects are limited to the number of stray animals the Spanish have left behind. It gives you a nice lifestyle now, but only a moderate future lies in breeding, for the use of the locals, in days to come."

"The ships will still need their supplies," Luke would reply.

"But those you are gathering around you to help you are not tied to you. They can easily take their knowledge of the trade and set up in rivalry.

"You need to find something that cannot be duplicated by any worker who is passing through."

At other times, Peter and his associates would relish their concept of true wealth.

"Wealth is power," they would say.

And Luke, shivering in the heat of a breathless night, would remind them:

"You can't take it with you when you die."

"But power is class. Your progeny will inherit a position in society that you can be proud to leave to them."

Chapter 15 – In the Shadows

Occasionally, during the conversations, Luke would glance at Zeesha in the shadows. He would suggest to his brother that family happiness now was more important than wealth in times to come.

Such public recognition of her presence angered Peter.

In private, he raved against it. He asked Luke to keep her away from visitors and remember her place.

Luke protested. He pointed to his need for her constant attention because of his sickness. But Peter said that, if he needed an attendant, he should have one who was not obviously pregnant.

Peter offered to buy him an African woman when the next ship came in.

Zeesha heard this with dismay. She withdrew further into herself. She feared for her baby.

She was too far from the cave mouth.

She had no wish to bring a new life to a place where they were buying and selling human beings.

She wondered whether the presence of another person would give her the chance to take one of the firearms to her people, unnoticed.

She felt she had discovered most of what there was to know about these people and their intentions. She had finally completed her task.

When the next ship came in, Peter bought a slave for Luke. She was to be Zeesha's substitute, in Luke's shadow. She was to care for him when the fever rose and give him soothing teas when he became delirious.

Zeesha was jealous, but proud. She instructed her in the use of the herbs from the goat-skin bag.

Peter explained the situation to his brother.

"You do realise that this malaria is unlikely to get better?" he began.

"You may have felt you were doing the right thing by heading for the hills. And by taking a native woman who could help you to survive.

"But I have been giving careful consideration to how wealth is created on other islands.

"I have taken my time and designed a home that will be airy, clean and fresh. I am taking workers who are hardened to the climate and bonded to me.

"Though I take my pleasure here, my family life will be in England, where wealth and respectability will ensure us a place at the top of society. I don't want you to threaten that.

"Luke, the people who visit here travel back and forth to England on a regular basis. Let us not parade what we do here before them. Keep your woman in the shadows. Let us safeguard our reputations."

Zeesha saw Luke tremble violently for some moments before replying:

"England provided nothing for us. That is why we fought in Cromwell's army. That is why we stayed here when we could have gone home. I have made a life for myself, and Zeesha has helped me."

Peter displayed the kind of tender tone that is only for the sick:

"Yes, you've made your life, and you've had your life. But your health has suffered irreparable damage, brother. Now, we can only keep you comfortable.

"I will not remove your child from you. However, we do not need to be embarrassed by the open partnership you have brought from the hills.

"Begin to put her from you."

Chapter 16 – The Ride

It was not long before Zeesha unwittingly played into Peter's hands.

She retreated from Luke's immediate company, but she could not give up the freedom she had enjoyed with him.

Luke had a horse called Bianco that was his pride and joy. Luke had relied on Zeesha to see to the animal's needs. She would exercise him whenever fever left Luke too weak to ride.

Zeesha had ridden Bianco, when she and Luke travelled to Peter's house.

Now, she needed to confer with her own people about the new turn of events.

She waited through long, hot days until the wind veered to blow inland from the sea, before she left the coastal dwellings to visit her people.

She set out early one evening. Visitors were being lavishly entertained by Peter and her absence from his house would be acceptable to him.

The horse, which had brought her from the hills, was amenable to the cool, sea breeze.

She thought that the odd dog, that noted her departure, would soon settle to gnawing discarded bones from the lavish table.

She rode swiftly on Bianco away from the swamp to the surrounding hills.

Yet, there was something unusual in the way the dogs were running and snapping at her horse's heels.

Zeesha gave Bianco his head. He pointed his nose towards the hills as if he knew her people awaited her there.

He stretched every tired muscle between every aching bone. His hoofs pounded in the dust as he strove to reach the distant line of trees.

It seemed he could sense her freedom was there.

Yet still, the dogs were following.

This was more than an evening's fun. They were running too far from the home of the man who fed them.

It was as if they were following her to seek out her intentions.

As she rode, she pondered.

She reviewed her relationship with Luke and its repression by Peter.

'Haven't I given them enough of *my time?*' she wondered to herself.

'*Does Luke think I won't go back in due time? I will go and show him the olive-skinned, dark almond-eyed, high-boned child I've formed from the happy days we've had.*

'*Does Luke think I won't? I'll dandle her on his knee. I'll let her grasp the ends of his hair and pull it*

*for the sheer joy of showing him she's
alive, and that he fathered her'*

The pounding of the little feet, still
within her womb, seemed to answer to
the pounding of Bianco's hooves.

Somewhere behind her was another
echo, at a lesser distance from the low,
white buildings than she was now.

The line of trees at the foot of the
hill was closer now. It was close enough
for her to distinguish the different
colours.

She wanted to slow down, even to
pause and look back at the coastal plain
where she had spent those few
revealing weeks.

But the barking of the following
dogs had become fearful and those

other hooves . . . they were no figment of her imagination, and they were too intense to be a recreational ride.

Luke must be following her.

Chapter 17 – Plausible Arguments

Now Zeesha began to feel afraid.

Many times she had looked at the Copperwright brothers and thought she was only there for a time.

When they made the move to Peter's settlement, Luke had bought a new horse for the journey – an English chestnut from along the coast.

She had laughed at his alarm when she had insisted on riding beside him on Bianco.

On those days when Luke felt strong, they used to ride together.

She had even rivalled him, joyfully galloping along the beach, trying to catch up with him on her older horse.

He had never seemed totally at ease with her challenge. But she had led him on to enjoy her company on his horse rides. And her companionship in his bed.

When she had begun to show more obvious signs of pregnancy, however, Luke joined with Peter to curtail her freedom, especially her riding.

Some of his arguments were plausible.

Bianco was too old to ride.

No, she could not borrow his other horse – the chestnut was too fresh.

Her old mount might stumble on a loose stone. She might fall and shake the baby. Was she such an irresponsible mother, to endanger a new life?

She had laughed until hard lines showed on his brother's face. She had felt brave and determined.

Now she was using Luke's horse to defy him.

Stay in the back of the house! Don't be seen by our guests until you have delivered that child!

That was what she was running from.

She started to push the grey to his limit. The pounding was in her head as well now.

Deliver a child in a house that used people for forced labour?

Live surrounded by men who considered her liaison shameful?

Amongst what kind of people?

Rough-necks who had sailed from England with the invading force? Who now gathered to Peter's call, from other islands along the way?

Stay with that ragged band? Their knowledge of tropical hygiene was nil. No one amongst them knew the healing properties of the herbs she might need.

Would she have to chance her life and her baby's life to the hands of one or two old women?

Those women had been picked up from the kitchens and back verandas of the Spanish town.

They had been left behind, considered too old and feeble to sail with the Spanish flotilla. They would be of no use to their masters when they reached Cuba.

Or would they send her to the agricultural land? That was where the African women worked, in hardship, longing for their homeland.

No! She would not submit to any of this.

Chapter 18 – The Return

Zeesha was on her way home to the caves that hid her people, whether the Copperwrights wanted her to go or not.

The grey slowed. Low branches and twigs began to tangle in her hair. But the dogs had not turned back and the drumming hooves behind her drew nearer.

She would have to turn to face it out with Luke.

She would have to try the teasing tactics that had always stood her in good stead since she had first seen him.

She would have to make him laugh. She would walk with him a little. She would lead him on, in and out of the trees. Then she would slip away.

Zeesha drew rein, and waited for Luke to come up, surrounded by his dogs.

Her eyes pierced the gloom that separated them. She was poised to meet him.

Suddenly she thought that perhaps night fevers were wracking him as he rode. Her compassion formed words of encouragement.

However, emerging from the

darkness was not Luke, but Peter Copperwright.

He sat sharply upright on his horse. His face was a mask of cruelty.

His eyes jeered.

"You have decided not to comply, so I am taking you back," he stated flatly.

Zeesha tried to fend off the veiled threat.

"You know I would have come back anyway. I just took a ride out while you were busy."

"Our business is no concern of yours. You are above yourself. Turn and ride ahead of me."

"I am not ready," she ventured.

Chapter 19 – The Dogs

Peter Copperwright said something to his dogs, and they snarled and snapped round Bianco's heels. The old horse laid back his ears. He kicked out and twitched his skin.

Zeesha tried to urge him in the direction of the hills but he would not move.

Peter Copperwright circled behind her. He flicked at the dogs with his whip. They jumped and grabbed at her heels, too.

They seethed around the horse. They snarled, their teeth to the horse's muzzle when he bucked, their jaws to his tail when he reared.

Zeesha almost lost her balance.

"Don't endanger the baby you bear," ordered Peter, cold and calm. "It is my brother's."

She was dizzy with fear. Bianco sensed her dismay and his nerve broke.

He reared again. He leapt off on his rear hooves, neck outstretched, ears flat, and bolted. He ran for the low, white homestead he had left behind.

Zeesha had to cling on tightly and bend low over the stretched neck. She was afraid that branches would unseat her and leave her as prey to the pursuing dogs.

The dogs were in full flight now, baying, and snarling at her mount.

The blood-curdling cries left her in no doubt of her fate if the horse stumbled and she fell.

Bianco's headlong career brought them back from the foot-hills.

They rode over the newly prepared cane fields, up the drive to the homestead, and into the yard behind it.

The horse swerved but showed no hesitation. He did not slow until the outhouses caused him to skid to a sudden halt.

It sent Zeesha sliding down his neck.

She coiled in a protective ball around her pregnancy. She rolled, to ease the impact of her fall.

Panting dogs slathered and snapped menacingly at her ears, her elbows and her fingertips.

She felt Peter's stinging lashes catch at her back, as he whipped the dogs away from the horse.

He continued whipping as he called for the three female slaves. They helped Zeesha to her feet.

"You are not fit to be one of them," he snarled. "You spy! Traitor! Rebel! I do not keep you by choice but just to minimise my brother's distress.

"If you were mine, I'd cut that child from your body and feed the rest of you to my dogs.

"But since you are his, you shall remain a slave until its birth.

"When the child is identified as my possession, my brother can do whatever ever he wills with you – while he lives, that is."

At that moment, Zeesha felt the pinnacle of despair and bitterness.

Her child was to be enslaved. Her freedom was curtailed. Her chosen man was dying.

She cared little what became of her. She allowed the slave women to guide her away.

Chapter 20 – Fight for Freedom

When her time came, the slave women were knowledgeable and compassionate midwives. They showered both mother and baby with affection.

But when she tried to tell them of life in the hills, they became silent and wary.

They related as much as they could of the cruelties they had suffered since leaving their country.

They needed time, they indicated, to build trust and unity among the different nations of Africa, who were being mingled indiscriminately on the new estates.

Zeesha was not entirely a slave, but neither was she entirely free.

She knew the lie of the land and how to conceal herself within it.

She was tied to the estate because her child had been born to slavery.

She was tied to the people of the uplands because she was their first ambassador for freedom.

Zeesha had given the 'zemi' to one of the slave women who had helped her give birth.

The woman who had received the gift of the 'zemi' watched Zeesha's movements carefully.

She concluded that the precious gift symbolised Zeesha's fight for freedom.

After her child was born Zeesha came and went in the shadows.

She knew that there was a future for the free people of her land, but she shared the sorrow of the enslaved.

Characters in the story

<u>The free people of the Uplands:</u>

Zeesha   an adolescent girl

Quashy   Zeesha's father, a wise
                and thoughtful man

Esther   Zeesha's ancestor – an
                inspiration to her people

Quincy   Husband of Esther - an
                ancestor of the people,
                fearless and far sighted

Ku   Leader of the Council.
                Quashy's younger brother
                and Zeesha's uncle

Koyot   Leader of the Warriors.
                Quashy's younger brother
                and Zeesha's uncle

<u>**The incomers from England**</u> – former soldiers in Oliver Cromwell's defeated army:

Luke Copperwright

> Father of Zeesha's child

Peter Copperwright

> Luke's elder brother – hostile to Zeesha

Bianco   Luke's horse

Author's Note:

Zeesha's story is a small fragment of my much longer novel entitled "Hues of Blackness".

That novel came out of a ten-year dialogue with Eva Jones, archivist of Savanna-la-Mar, Westmoreland, Jamaica.

She defined herself as a product of both her history and her home.

I first met Miss Eva more than twenty years ago, on Heroes Day, when I watched her receive an award for services to the parish. I was drawn by her erect dignity and fascinated by her wisdom.

A decade followed of conversations, writing, mentorship, hospitality and bracing friendship. I began to weave stories that would express her perspectives and her solutions to life's challenges.

In "Hues of Blackness" I allow each unique character to reveal herself from a different historical perspective. I have woven these women through time, so that no one will attach present or past personalities to them.

Miss Eva told me how her great-grandfather bought the family land over one hundred years ago. She had felt drawn to come back to it after a period abroad.

Later, she struggled hard to pay her siblings for their portion of the inheritance. She wanted to care for it, develop it, and hand it down to her daughter and grand-daughter.

The property is a stone's throw away from Savanna-la-Mar's parish council building. It is just across the road from St George's Parish Church and in full sight of the police station.

When Miss Eva was growing up, the bell of the parish church stood just outside her front gate. It was on top of a coaching shed that was designed to shelter horses. It also protected the gigs that the wealthy drove to church.

To the west of her home stretched the swamp. It was alive with small crabs. The whole area was veiled in tall, succulent, swamp grasses.

The land had been chosen by Adolphus Williams. He was the third son of a resident of Black River. He wanted the land for his wife, Ann Foote, and their three sturdy sons.

One son died young, despite his promising stature. Another was drawn to migrate by the opportunities of early emancipation days in the 1860s. So only one son remained in Westmoreland to continue the family name.

He married Ann Pennycook from Flower Hill. She was a descendant of famous brothers who had fought in Cromwell's army in the English civil war. They had received land in Westmoreland and two neighbouring parishes, as rewards for their services.

Sadly, Eva Jones died in February 2009. My novel is dedicated to her memory. And to the continuation of the understandings she shared during her lifetime.

R.T.P.